My Barn

CRAIG BROWN

Greenwillow Books, New York

Pastels and pen-and-ink were used for the full-color art.
The text type is ITC Zapf International Medium.

Printed in Singapore by Tien Wah Press
First Edition
1 2 3 4 5 6 7 8 9 10

Library of Congress Cataloging-in-Publication Data
Brown, Craig McFarland.
My barn / by Craig Brown.
p.   cm.
Summary: Each of the animals inhabiting the barn
makes sounds that distinguish it from the others.
ISBN 0-688-08785-X (trade).
ISBN 0-688-08786-8 (lib.)
[1. Animal sounds—Fiction.
2. Domestic animals—Fiction.
3. Barns—Fiction.]   I. Title.
PZ7.B81287Bar   1991
[E]—dc20   90-41758   CIP   AC

For Jane L. Brown,
wonderful teacher
and mother

I like the sound

ER ER ER ER ERRRRR ER ERERER ERRR...

the sound that a rooster makes.

I like the sound

RUFF RUFF RUUUUFFF RUFF RUFF RUUUFF...

the sound a dog makes.

I like the sound

BUK BUK BUK BUKK BUKK BUK BUKKK BUK...

the sound a chicken makes.

I like the sound

MOO MMMMOOOOHH MOOHHH MMOOOO…

the sound a cow makes.

I like the sound

MEOW MEOOOOWWW MEOW MEOOOWWWW...

the sound a cat makes.

I like the sound

HONK HONK HOOONK HONNNK HONK HONK...

the sound a goose makes.

I like the sound

GOBBLE GOBBLE GOBBLLE GOBBLE GOBBLE...

the sound a turkey makes.

I like the sound
WHOO WHOOOOOO WHOOOO WHOO WHOO...
the sound an owl makes.

I like the sound

OINK OOOOINK OINNNK OINK OINK...

the sound a pig makes.

I like the sound
BAHAHAHA BAHAHAHAHA BAH BAH BAHAHA...
the sound a sheep makes.

I like the sound

HEE HAWWW HEEE HAWW HEE HAW...

the sound a donkey makes.

I like the sound

PEEP PEEP PEEEP PEEEP PEEP PEEP PEEP PEEP...

the sound baby chicks make.

I like the sound

WHEHEE WHEEHEHEHEEE WHEHEHEEEHE...

the sound a horse makes.

I like the sound
BUZZ BUZZ BUZZZZZZ BUUZZZZ BUZZ BUZZ...
the sound a bee makes.

I love all the sounds…
all the sounds on my farm.